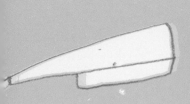

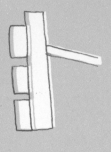

First published in 2011 by Child's Play (International) Ltd
Ashworth Road, Bridgemead, Swindon SN5 7YD

Distributed in USA by Child's Play Inc
250 Minot Avenue, Auburn, Maine 04210

Distributed in Australia by Child's Play Australia Pty Ltd
Unit 10/20 Narabang Way, Belrose, NSW 2085

Text and illustrations copyright © Claudia Boldt 2011
The moral right of the author/illustrator has been asserted

ISBN 978-1-84643-372-6
CLP120810CPL12103726

Printed and bound in Shenzhen, China
1 3 5 7 9 10 8 6 4 2

A catalogue record of this book is available from the British Library

www.childs-play.com

Slug was very upset.

This was *always* happening.

"Why, oh why, does no one like me?"

Today had been particularly bad. Slug felt that the whole world thought he was ugly.

Spider heard Slug sobbing.

"Why are you so sad?" she asked.

"Oh, it's nothing," said Slug.

"Boohooooo! Nothing."

"Nothing must be very sad," said Spider.

When he looked up,
Slug screamed with horror.
Spider was not impressed.
"Oh dear," she said.
"You are so very impolite."
But when Slug dared to look at
her again, Spider was smiling.

Slug decided he would speak to Spider.
After all, nobody else had ever bothered
to ask him why he was sad.
"Boohoooo! It's because I am so ugly,"
he cried. "When I was young, I thought
I would grow up to be a butterfly or
at least a snail. Little did I know that...
Boohoohooo!"

"Don't be silly," said Spider. "Most people
are scared of me because they think I'm ugly!"

"So why aren't you crying?" asked Slug.

"Because I know I'm not ugly!"

"Aren't you?" asked Slug.

"No," said Spider. "I am extraordinarily beautiful!"

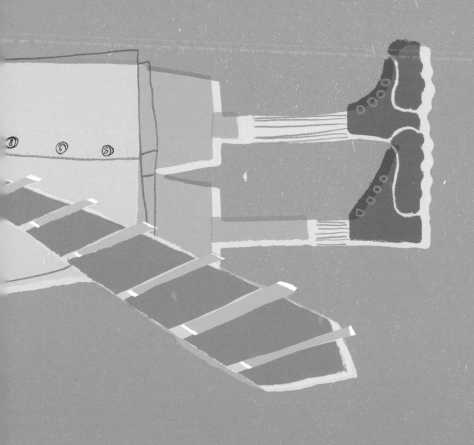

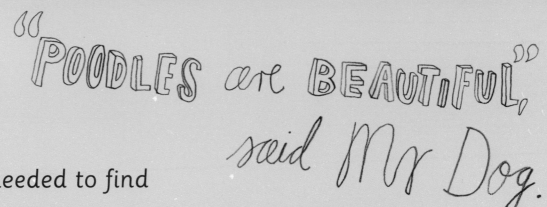

"POODLES are BEAUTIFUL," said Mr Dog.

Slug decided he needed to find out what 'beautiful' really was.

He went to see his cousin, Leech, and asked him.

"Red is beautiful," replied Leech. Now Slug was really confused.

He asked other people what else was beautiful, but everybody gave him a different answer.

"My beautiful big furry coat."

"My big tummy is beautiful."

"My singing is extraordinarily beautiful."

"Only

words

can

be

beautiful."

"Beauty is
in the eye of
the bee-holder."

"The postman."

"My behind."

"L O N G is beautiful!"

"This is terrible!" complained Slug.

"Nobody thinks that I'm beautiful."

"I think you're beautiful," said Spider.

"Are you serious?" Slug was flattered.

"What a lovely looking slug," interrupted a passing hedgehog.

"Why, thank you!" said Slug. "Do you really mean me?"

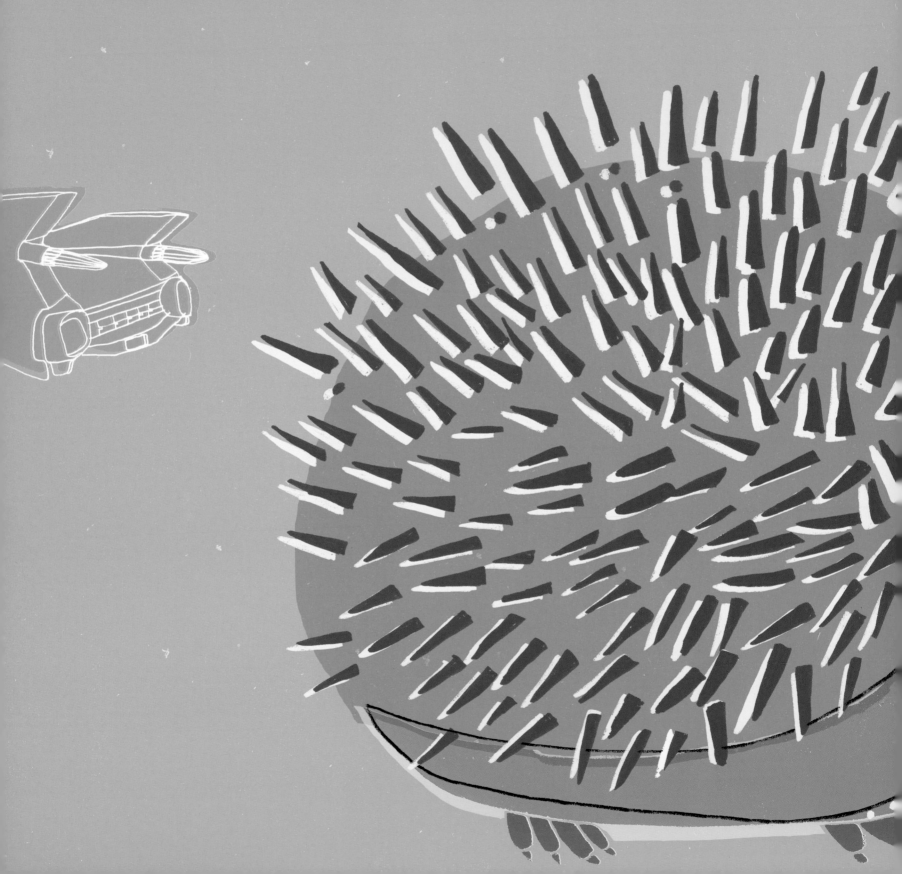

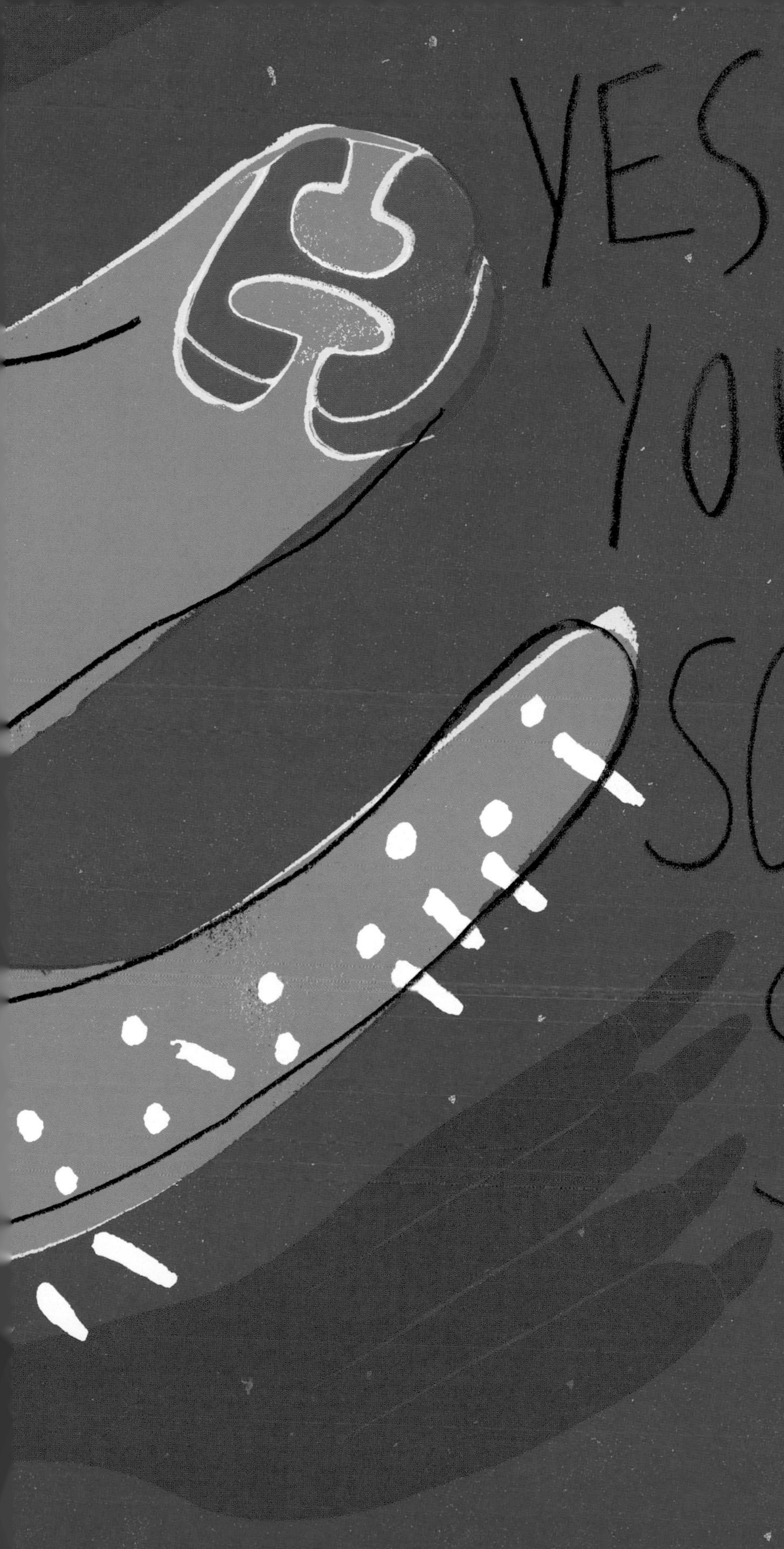

YES, I MEAN YOU. SO BIG. SO SWEET. SO JUICY.

"It's nice up here, isn't it?" asked Spider.

"Yes," said Slug. "It's beautiful."

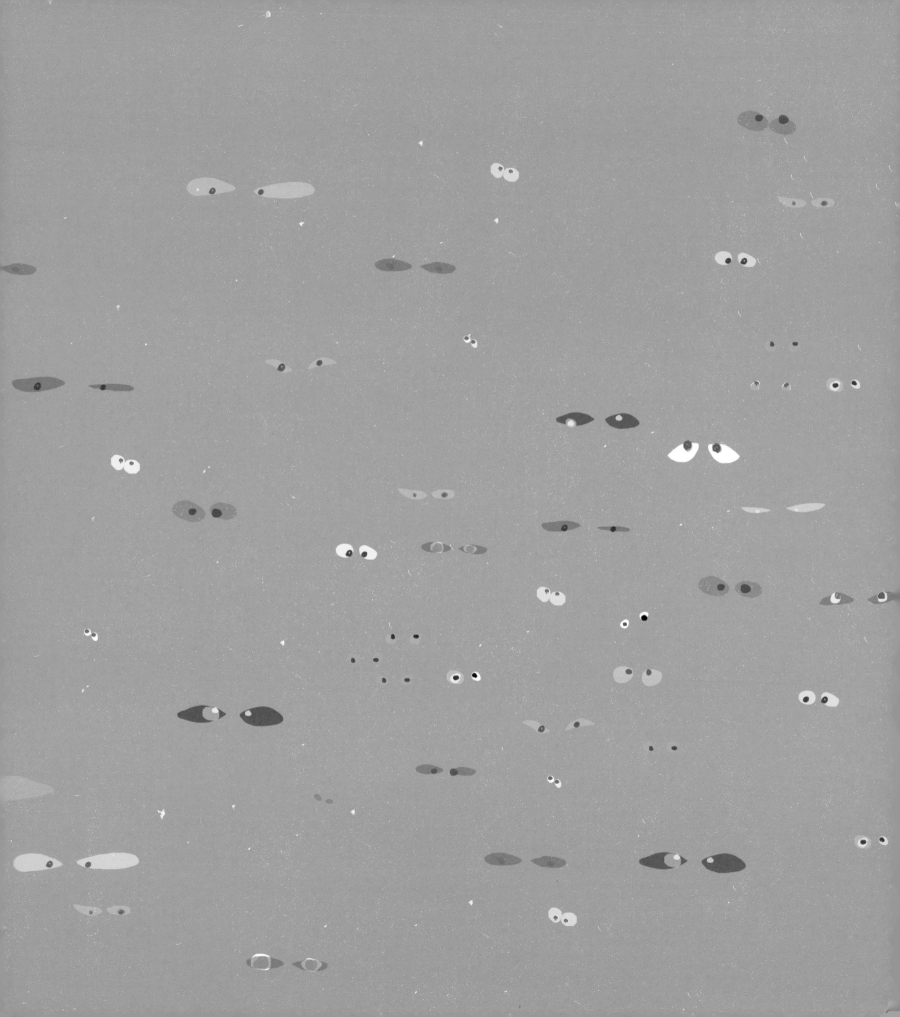